# MOONSTRUCK

## The True Story of the Cow Who Jumped Over the Moon

### Gennifer Choldenko
### Illustrated by Paul Yalowitz

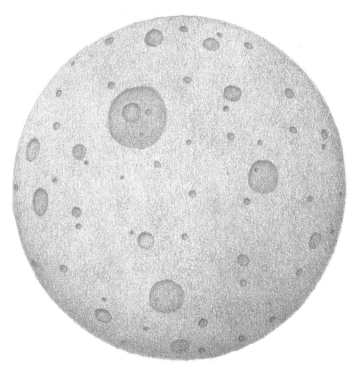

Hyperion Books for Children
New York

Text © 1997 by Gennifer Choldenko.
Illustrations © 1997 by Paul Yalowitz.

Printed in Hong Kong by South China Printing Company (1988) Ltd.

First Edition

1 3 5 7 9 10 8 6 4 2

The artwork for each picture is prepared using colored pencil.

This book is set in 16-point ITC Usherwood.

Library of Congress Cataloging-in-Publication Data
Choldenko, Gennifer, (date)
Moonstruck: The true story of the cow who jumped over the moon. / by Gennifer Choldenko ;
illustrated by Paul Yalowitz.
—1st ed.
p.    cm.
Summary: The horse seriously doubts that the cow will ever be able
to jump over the Moon but offers respect and admiration when the
determined bovine accomplishes that feat.
ISBN 0-7868-0158-1 (trade) — ISBN 0-7868-2130-2 (lib. bdg.)
[1. Horses—Fiction.  2. Cows—Fiction.  3. Moon—Fiction.]
I. Yalowitz, Paul, ill.  II. Title.
PZ7.C446265Mo    1996
[E]—dc20                      95-14846

To my dad, James Alexander Johnson
—G. C.

For Dad, Mom, and Sara Lou, too
—P. Y.

**Mother Goose** . . . what a bag of feathers she is. She makes it sound so easy. Nine hundred forty-one pounds of cow meat, not counting the udder, catapults 240,000 miles to jump over the moon—and what does that old goose woman write? One lousy line—not even a whole poem. I know for a fact the cow was hurt by it, but who am I to say? I'm just an old brown horse. Only *then* I was a young brown horse.

Anyway, I'm getting ahead of myself. I want to tell you the whole story.

First of all, you may not know this, but we horses jump over the moon on a regular basis.  Every night at least one of us makes the trip. I don't want to make it sound easy or anything, but we all do it. We can handle it. We're built for it. We begin training from a very early age.

Which is just what we were doing when this cow started hanging around. At first she kept her distance. And, to be quite honest, we were kind of flattered. Who doesn't like an audience?

Then she started trying to get friendly. Asking dumb questions like, "Do you take a running start?"  I mean, come on. Whoever heard of jumping clear over the moon from a dead standstill?

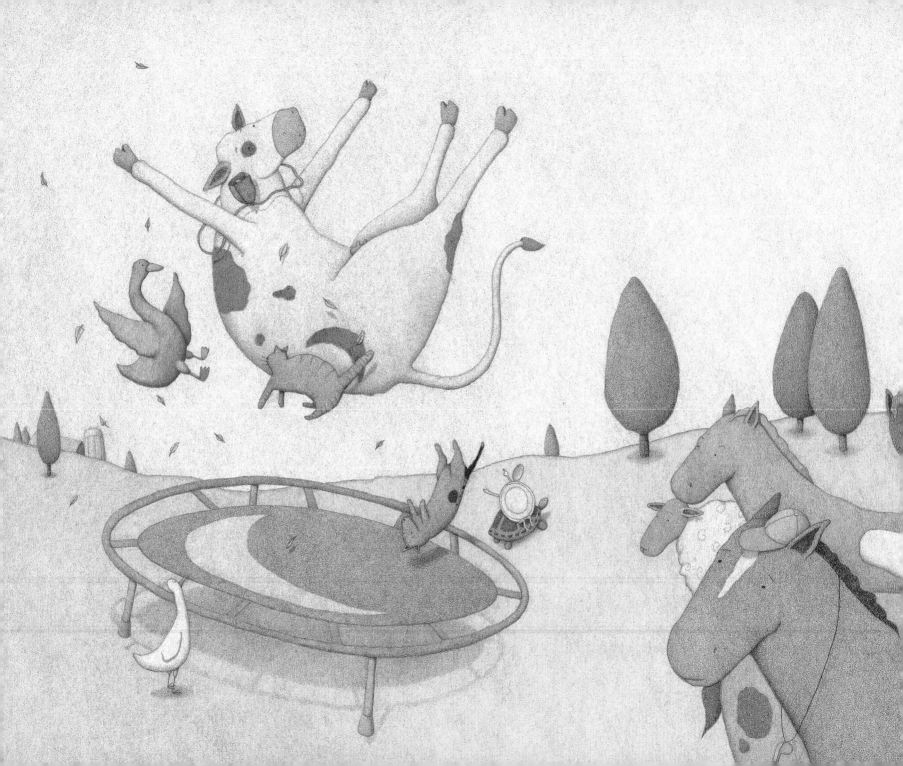

Every day she was there, cold weather or warm. As if that weren't bad enough, she began using our equipment herself. That's when I knew I had to have a talk with that cow. I mean, let's face it. Not everyone can be born a horse.

"Look, kid," I said to the cow, "you can't keep doing this. You're going to get hurt. Why don't you go chew the cud with your cow friends?"

"No," she said. "I'm going to jump the moon."

"Honey, come on!  You're a cow. Take a look at that body of yours . . . those short little legs, that galumphing stride . . ."

"I don't care," she said. "I'm going to. Every night I look up and say to myself, One day I'm going to see what the moon looks like up close. One day I'm going to jump clear over that moon."

Now I understood. This cow was MOON-STRUCK! There was no use trying to talk sense to her.

"Okay, kid," I said, "I'll give you a shot. But if you can't keep up, you're out. Is that a deal?"

"It's a deal," she said.

I didn't mention this to the others. What—
I'm going to tell them I recruited a *cow* for
the team?  I figured she wouldn't last longer
than a day or two anyway. Then we'd be rid
of her for good.

Boy, was I wrong.

First thing in the morning, there she was.
Last thing at night . . . still there.

Every time I'd get ready to tell her to head back to her herd, she'd go and do something really well and I'd have to keep my mouth shut for another day. After a few months, she was jumping as well as the quarter horses. Then what could I say?

So that's how it went for most of the season until we got down to the final part of the training: the Wall.

Some of the horses sweat the nails right out of their shoes when it's their turn to jump the Wall.  There was no way a cow could clear it, no matter how hard she tried. But when I told the cow that, she galloped off, all in a huff—and I didn't see her again until I was setting up flags for the Wall.

Then all of a sudden there she was, thundering toward the Wall, her cowbell clanking wildly.

"No!" I hollered as the cow gathered her legs under her and sprang all the way over the great stone hurdle.

"Yes! Yes!" the horses shouted, stamping their hooves in salute to that black-and-white babe.

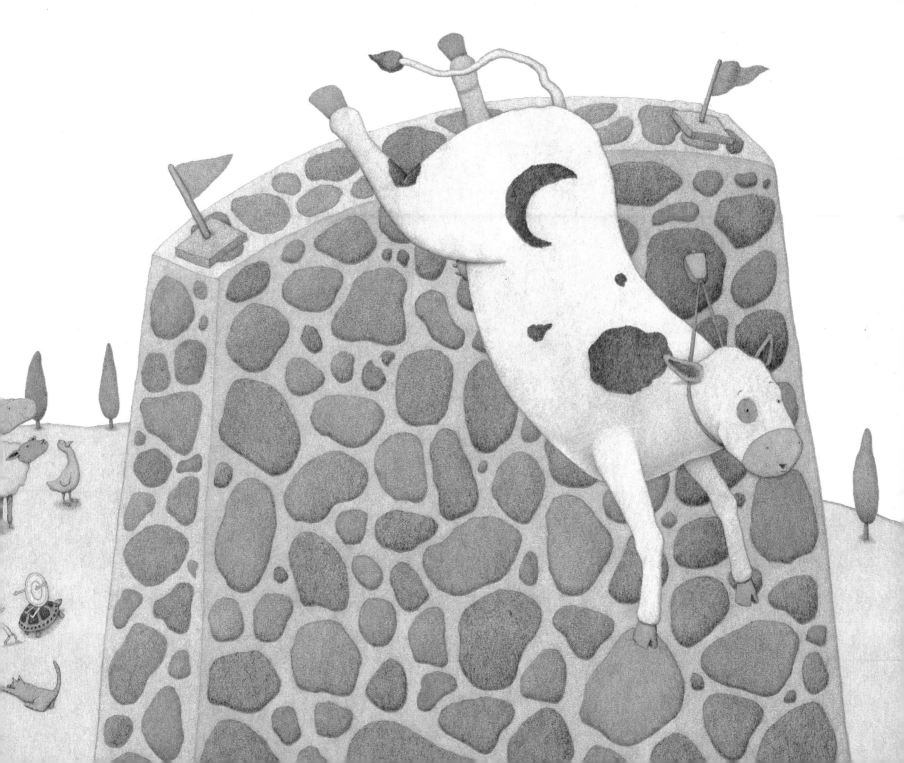

After that, I have to tell you, I had to rethink the whole cow thing. Some years half my horses can't clear the Wall and here this crazy bovine jumped it first time out. So that very day I posted a list of the horses who were ready to jump the moon. And on the list I included the cow.

When the cow found out she'd been chosen, you could hear her mooing from one end of the farm to the other. She was so excited, she could hardly keep her mind on schooling those last few days.

But when the night came for her to jump, she was calm and confident, her mind focused on flight.

10, 9, 8, 7, 6, 5, 4, 3, 2, 1 . . . BLAST OFF!
and she burst forward down the hill.

Faster and faster the cow galloped down the hill. Faster and faster she went as she gathered her legs under her and rocketed into the night.

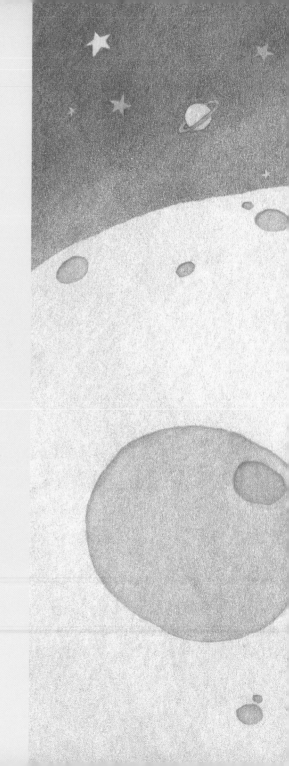

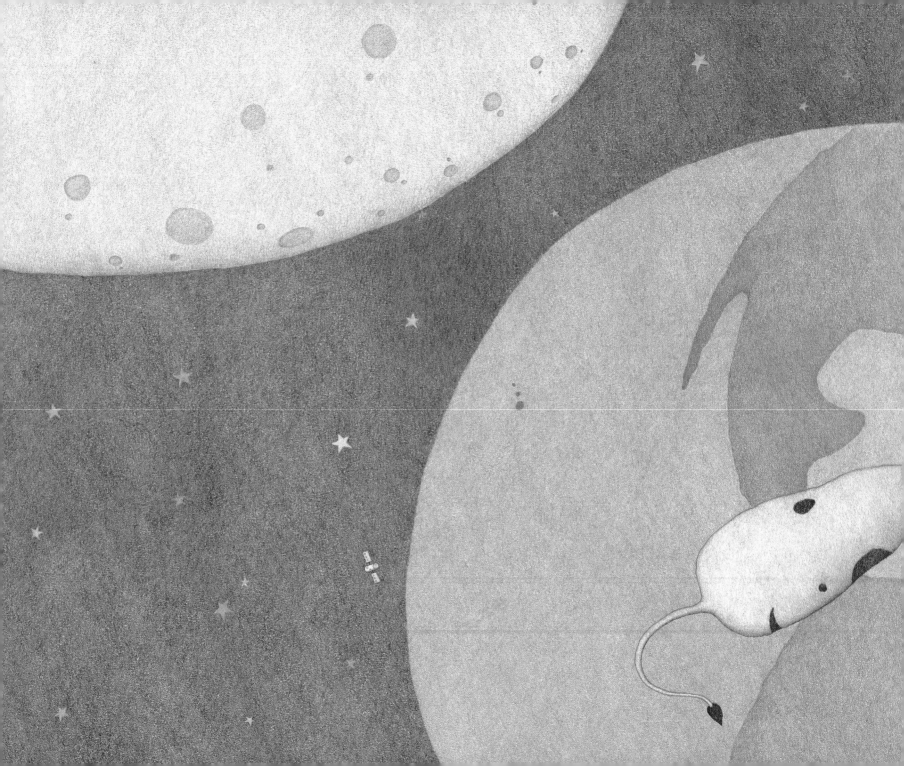

Higher and higher the cow flew, careening through space at an incredible speed.

Up and up and up until one, two, three, all four of her stubby legs soared past that big old moon. And then around and around and up and over until she'd seen every bit of the moon up close. And the stars and meteorites and the Milky Way and the Earth . . . And then when there was nothing left to see, gently, gently, gravity brought her back to Earth again.

Well, I can tell you that when she came back, there wasn't a dry eye on the whole planet. Which is why I know for certain that old Mother Goose wasn't around. Because if she'd seen that holstein jump the moon with her own eyes, she wouldn't be wasting her time writing about cats and fiddles and the courtship of dishes and spoons. She would have written a whole book about that cow.

Published exclusively for Nordstrom by Chronicle Books LLC.

Text © 2007 by Nordstrom, Inc.
Illustrations © 2007 by Lisa Evans.

All rights reserved.

Book design by Margo Sepanski and Maria Blackburn.
Lisa Evans illustrations provided by Folioart at www.folioart.co.uk.

ISBN 978-0-8118-6269-1
Manufactured in USA.

10 9 8 7 6 5 4 3 2 1
Chronicle Books LLC
680 Second Street, San Francisco, CA 94107

www.chroniclebooks.com

NORDSTROM

ONCE UPON A HOLIDAY

The Moon Fell Out of the Sky

Written by Randy Schliep

Illustrated by Lisa Evans

chronicle books · san francisco

Once upon a time, on a snowy Christmas Eve, a little girl named Sophie had just moved with her mother and father into an old house at the edge of the forest. Her only friends were some stuffed toys and the moon outside her window. Moon visited her every night and she told him her deepest secrets, like how hard it was to move away from her old house and her friends. She even told Moon about her letter to Santa Claus, and how this year there was only one wish in it—a new friend to play with.

Not far away, under the very same moon, lived an exceptional cow named Lily. She had a wish of her own—to be the first cow to jump over that moon. And so it was, on this magical Christmas Eve, wearing nothing but a bicycle helmet, a good-luck scarf and a goofy grin, that a lowly cow with high ambition prepared to leap into the moonlit sky.

With all her animal friends lining the makeshift runway, Lily lumbered
into a galloping run. Then she shut her eyes and jumped!

When Lily opened her eyes, she was higher than she ever dreamed! Higher than the barn. Higher than the windmill. Higher even than the highest trees in the forest.

Soon Lily was soaring among the stars. It was like swimming in a sea of diamonds. Millions upon millions. Then suddenly there was Moon, coming right at Lily like a ball toward a bat.

The impact knocked Moon out of his orbit, and the next thing he knew he was zooming down, down, down. Lily was falling, too, spinning and tumbling as the snow-covered ground rushed up to meet them both.

Luckily for Lily and Moon, they landed in a fresh snowbank in Sophie's backyard. The muffled *thump-thump* woke a sleepy Sophie from her slumber. She rubbed her eyes and peered out the window. She saw one hole in the snow shaped like a cow and another shaped like a perfect circle. A shaft of shimmering light rose eerily from the circle, illuminating the curiously dark night sky.

Sophie could hardly believe her eyes. She quickly bundled up and slipped outside to investigate. A big white owl perched on a low tree limb watched her as she plowed her way through the powdery snow.

"What happened?" Sophie wondered out loud.

"It was a lunar catastrophe of bovine proportions! It was *udderly* horrifying," said Owl.

"You can talk," Sophie whispered in amazement.

"Of course!" hooted Owl. "After all, I am the wisest creature in the forest."

"It was an accident!" came an excited shout from the cow-shaped hole. "I meant to jump *over* the moon."

"Who is that?" asked Sophie as she walked toward the voice.

"It's me, Lily!" moooed the cow. "Could you please help me out of this hole? I'm so cold, my milk is turning into ice cream!"

"*You* can talk, too!" cried Sophie as she and Owl reached down to lend a hand to the shivering cow.

"Perfect!" scolded Owl. "Now perhaps you can tell us how Santa will be able to deliver toys tonight with no moonlight to guide his way?"

"Owl's right!" gasped Sophie. "What are we going to do?"

Sophie looked from Owl to Lily and up at the inky black space in the sky where Moon once shone, and she knew this was going to be a very unusual Christmas Eve indeed.

Up at the North Pole, Santa had noticed the change in the night sky, too.
It was black as pitch. "What in the world has happened to Moon?"
Santa wondered. There wasn't a worse time for such a thing to happen.
After all, it was Christmas Eve and there were billions of presents to deliver.
Santa's jolly thoughts instantly turned into worries—and he began to pace.

ophie, Lily and Owl wondered if Moon would ever smile down on them from the sky again. They watched as his eyes slowly opened.

"What happened?" asked Moon. "I have a terrible headache."

"You were knocked out of the sky by a cow," hooted Owl.

Sophie leaned forward so Moon could see her better. "This is the cow, and her name is Lily, and she is terribly, terribly sorry. And this is Owl, the smartest creature in the forest, and I'm Sophie—you landed in my yard."

"I know you, young lady," said Moon. "You're the little girl who talks to me every night."

The three helped Moon out of his perfectly round hole and dusted the powdery snow off his face.

"I know you, too," Moon said to Owl. "You stay up from dusk 'til dawn."

"I even know this silly cow," Moon said as he patted Lily on her back. "She sleeps standing up. I know you all, and I would love to stay and chat, but I need to get back home—Santa will be making his deliveries tonight, and he needs me to light his way."

"I will help you," hooted Owl. "I am the wisest creature in the forest, and I shall think and think and think until I come up with a way to get you back up into the sky where you belong."

"Me too," added Sophie.

"Me too," moooed Lily.

And with that, the little group thought and thought and thought.

Suddenly Owl said, "I've got it! We can make a helicopter out of Sophie's lawnmower. We can remove the engine, turn it upside down and bolt it to a hat. The spinning blades will fly Moon straight up into the sky, and he'll be home in no time. It's a brilliant plan, very wise indeed."

"Udder genius," agreed the cow.

"Well, I don't know," said Sophie. "I don't know how to build a helicopter hat from a lawnmower. Do either of you?"

"Well, no," said Owl, "but I built a nest once."

"I can't even floss my teeth, much less turn a screwdriver!" moooed Lily. "With nothing but hooves to work with, I'm as clumsy as an ox."

"We have to keep thinking," said Sophie.

"All right," hooted Owl. "There are other solutions, I am sure. So I shall think of one of them. Something even better!"

And so Owl thought some more. Sophie thought, too, and so did Lily, but it was Owl who hooted first.

"This is for the birds!" he said.

"It certainly is," groaned Moon.

"It's ridiculous," agreed Lily.

"For the *birds*?" asked Sophie.

"Indeed!" declared Owl. "I shall ask all my fine feathered friends to tie strings around their feet and around Moon's arms. Then together they can give Moon a lift home."

"But what if they fly south instead of up?" asked Sophie.

"Ah, good thinking," said Owl. "Then Moon would be vacationing on a beach instead of sitting on his perch in the night sky. I shall ponder another solution."

And so Owl closed his big eyes and thought some more.

"I have it!" exclaimed Owl. "We shall shoot Moon from a cannon. He is shaped just like a cannon ball. All we have to do is find a cannon big enough to hold him."

"Where will we find a cannon at this time of night?" moooed Lily.

"And what about the noise? We'll wake everybody up for miles around," said Sophie.

"Yes, yes. Too true," muttered Owl. "Back to the drawing board."

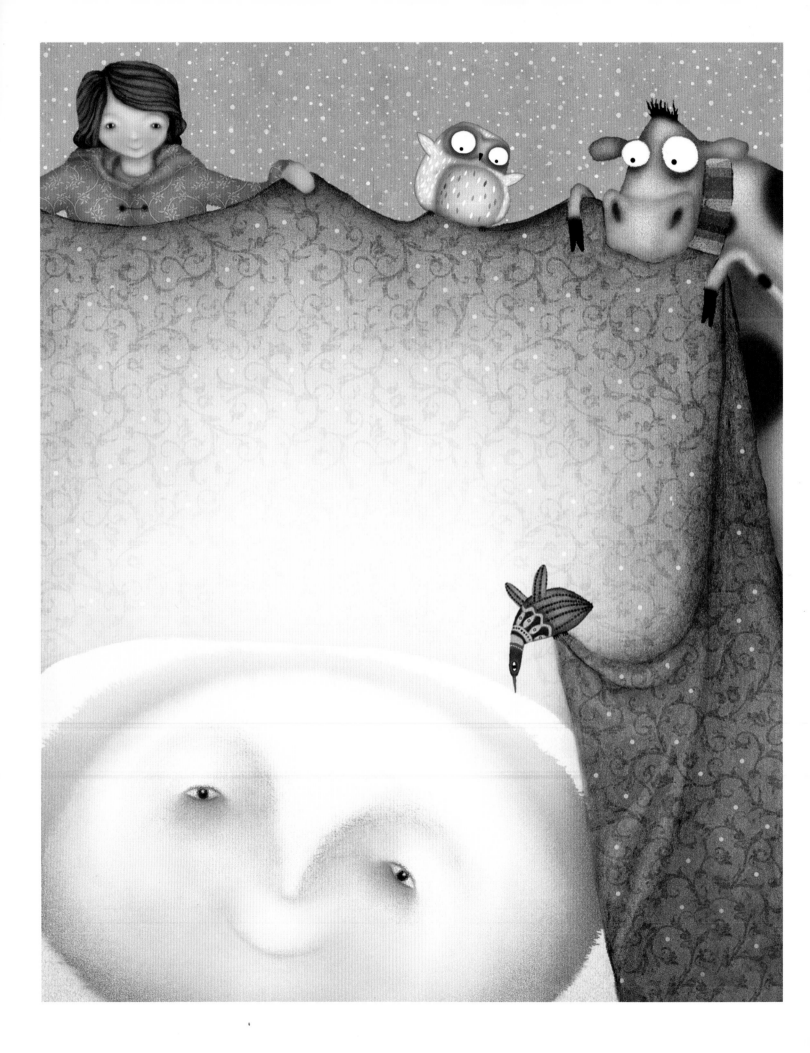

"I know just what we can do," said Sophie thoughtfully. Everyone turned to her. "What if we got Santa to take Moon back in his sleigh? He's going to be flying through the sky tonight, so all we have to do is signal him to land here. Once we explain the problem, I'm sure he'll help. What do you think, Owl? Is that a wise idea?"

"Why, it's so wise I can't believe I didn't think of it myself."

"It's absolutely brilliant!" moooed Lily.

"Sophie," smiled Moon, "your idea is as bright as . . . well . . . me!"

"But how shall we contact Santa?" asked Owl.

"He'll be flying so high in the sky!" said Lily.

"And it will be too dark for him to see us if we try to wave him down," said Owl.

"Well," said Sophie, "maybe we can use Moon's light to beam a signal to Santa. We can cover and uncover Moon with my quilt, and maybe Santa will come to investigate the flashing light!"

With that, she clapped her hands in excitement and dashed back to her room to get the quilt from her bed.

Moon rolled back into the hole where he'd landed and concentrated all his light into one powerful moonbeam that he shot high into the sky. With a little help from her friends, Sophie covered and uncovered Moon's bright light over and over until her arms grew so tired, she could barely lift the blanket one more time.

Back at the top of the world, Santa Claus was loading his sleigh with bags of toys. Without Moon's light, he didn't know how he would find his way. But he knew he had to try. After all, it was Christmas Eve. Santa wrapped his coat around himself, kissed Mrs. Claus and climbed into his sleigh. He snapped the reigns and began to shout, "On Dasher, on Dancer, on Prancer, on Vixen . . . ," and up into the dark night sky he flew.

At first it was so dark, Santa couldn't see a thing. Then suddenly he spied a blinking light on the horizon.

"That doesn't look like starlight. What could it be?" wondered Santa.

"Comet! Cupid! Donner! Blitzen! Look below! Maybe we've found the answer to the mystery of this dark Christmas Eve night."

With that, Santa turned his reindeer toward the mysterious light.

In Sophie's backyard, Moon peeked from behind the quilt. "I sure hope this works!" he said.

"It did! It did!" yelled Lily, pointing to the sky.

Santa's magical sleigh swooped down and he landed with a spray of fluffy snow and a hearty "Ho, ho, ho!"

Sophie explained what happened and Santa happily agreed to take Moon back home. Sophie, Owl and Lily helped Santa load Moon into the sleigh, and with shouts of thanks, warm hugs and waving arms, Santa and Moon flew back into the star-filled sky.

Sophie shook her quilt free of snow and folded it in her arms.

"Young lady," hooted Owl, "you helped the moon get home and saved Christmas as well. I shall never forget what you've done tonight. I don't know whooooo could've done better."

"I have never been so moooved," smiled Lily. "I can't thank you enough."

"I enjoyed meeting you both as well," said Sophie with a little curtsey. "But now I must go to bed. Santa will be coming, and I have to be asleep or he won't leave a present for me."

Sophie gave Lily a good-bye hug, blew a kiss up to Owl in his tree, then stamped the snow from her shoes before she stepped into the kitchen.

"I'll never forget this night," she thought as she sleepily climbed the stairs to her room.

Sophie was just slipping under her big, puffy quilt when suddenly her room filled with the warm glow of moonlight. She sat up and peered out the window. There was Moon, back in the sky where he belonged, his smiling face shining on Santa's sleigh as it made a big, lazy turn on its way back to earth.

Sophie fell contentedly into her fluffy pillow, visions of happy Christmas mornings swimming in her head as she drifted into a deep, cozy sleep.

The next morning when she awoke, Sophie smiled as she thought of the night before. Had a cow really knocked the moon out of the sky? She peeked out her window and saw that the snowy holes were still there! A bit melty now, but definitely there. "I did meet Moon, Lily and Owl," she whispered to herself. "And Santa came! So he must have brought a friend for me!"

Sophie climbed out of bed and rushed down the stairs. But her excitement faded when she saw that there was no friend waiting for her. In fact, it looked as if Santa had left no presents for her at all! Instead there was a silver box with a tag on it that read *For Veronica*. Who was Veronica? How could Santa Claus have made such a mistake?

Just then there was a knock at the front door. Sophie opened it, and there stood a little girl who looked exactly Sophie's age, holding a beautifully wrapped present.

"Hi, I'm Veronica. I live down the road. I think Santa left your present at my house by mistake. Is your name Sophie?"

"Yes, it is," said Sophie, smiling with excitement. "And I have your present. Santa must have gotten really mixed up last night. Do you want to stay and play?"

"I'd love to!" answered Veronica.

And that's how Sophie met her best friend ever—thanks to a silly cow,
a wise owl, a friendly moon and the magic of Christmas.